# AND THE LION

retold by Steven Otfinoski

illustrated by Gustavo Mazali

## TABLE OF CONTENTS

# CHAPTER ONE A FRIEND IN NEED

In Rome there once lived a slave named Androcles. The master who purchased him treated him poorly. One day Androcles took his few possessions and ran away. In a dark forest, he heard a loud roar.

"That sounds like a lion!" he thought.

He heard the roar again. Now it sounded more like a moan. In a clearing, he saw the lion. Androcles was frightened. But the lion didn't move.

The beast was in pain. Its right paw was bleeding. A large thorn was stuck in it.

Androcles could see that the lion was hurt. Androcles was scared, but he was brave. He walked step by step very slowly toward the lion. The lion didn't roar. He just looked up at Andocles and cried out in pain.

Androcles knew he had to help the lion.

Androcles looked at the lion's paw. He saw the thorn, and he gently pulled it out. Then he tore a piece of fabric from his clothes. He wrapped it around the hurt paw. The lion was grateful. He beamed at Androcles and licked his face.

Androcles patted the lion's mane and said, "Take it easy, and get some rest. Give your paw time to heal. Then you will be fine. You will be able to roam the forests and hunt for your own food once again."

Androcles bid the lion farewell and went on his way. After a long day of walking, he found a cave. He rested his head on a rock. Soon he fell sound asleep.

Androcles hadn't known it, but he had fallen asleep in one of the lion's caves. When he awoke, the lion was standing over him. The lion gave Androcles some food. Androcles hadn't realized how hungry he was. He ate the food and thanked the lion.

Then both Androcles and the lion fell asleep.

## CHAPTER TWO **THE CAPTURE**

Men's voices awakened Androcles. Soldiers were looking for him. He tried to warn the lion but it was too late. The soldiers entered the cave. They pointed their swords at Androcles. They threw a net over the lion.

"What will you do with me?" asked Androcles.

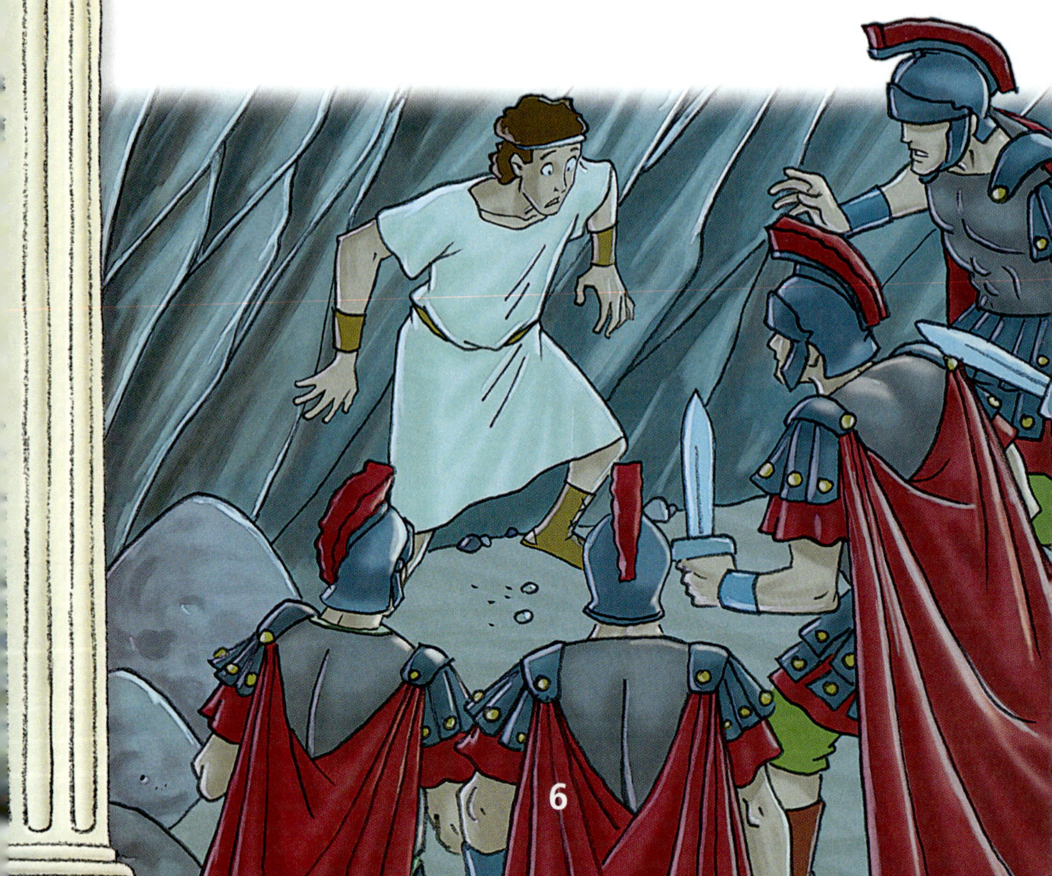

"The Emperor will decide," said the head soldier.

"What about the lion?" Androcles asked.

"We'll take him back with us as well," said the soldier.

"But he's done nothing wrong," argued Androcles.

"Silence, slave!" said another soldier.

So they marched Androcles and the lion to the city. There, they threw Androcles into prison.

## CHAPTER THREE **A FRIEND INDEED**

Many days passed, and Androcles was placed in an arena. The seats were filled. People were laughing, talking, and quarreling. Then the Emperor took his seat. Everyone was silent.

Bugles sounded. The crowd shouted with excitement. Some people stomped their feet. Some clapped their hands. They did not want to wait any longer.

"Let the games begin!" cried the Emperor.

Androcles looked up. He could not believe what he was looking at. Coming through an open door he saw his old friend, the lion!

The lion looked around. He roared. He was hungry. Suddenly he saw Androcles. He roared again and ran towards him.

Just as he was about to leap at Androcles, the lion stopped in his tracks. He circled Androcles, one, two times. The crowd got very quiet.

Then the lion licked his old friend's hand. Androcles smiled and patted the lion's mane.

The crowd had never seen such a thing. They became angry.

## CHAPTER FOUR **THE DECISION**

"What's wrong?" someone cried. "Why isn't that lion eating the slave?"

"Come here, slave," the Emperor said. "I want to talk to you."

Androcles bowed.

"Do you know why that lion didn't eat you?" the Emperor asked.

"Yes," said Androcles, "because he is my friend."

"Friend?" said the Emperor. "How could that be?"

Then Androcles told the story of how he had helped the lion.

The Emperor smiled and said, "Your kindness saved your life once. Now I will save it again. I will give you freedom. You may go wherever you want."

Androcles was thrilled. Then he thought of his friend.

"But what about the lion?" he asked.

"The lion is free, too," said the Emperor. "He may return to the forest."

And that is just what the lion did. But he never forgot his friend Androcles. And Androcles never forgot him.

# Comprehension Check

## Summarize

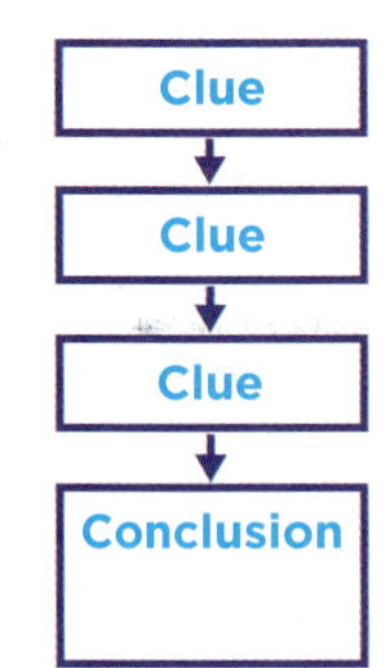


Use a Conclusion Map to form conclusions about important events in this story. Then summarize the story using the map.

## Think and Compare

1. Look back to pages 12–14. Why does the Emperor spare the life of Androcles and free him? ***(Draw Conclusions)***

2. What would you do if you came upon an animal that was hurt? Explain. ***(Evaluate)***

3. Why are bravery and kindness important traits for people to have? ***(Apply)***

Seymou

SEE

# PLANETS AROUND THE SUN

SCHOLASTIC INC.
New York Toronto London Auckland Sydney
Mexico City New Delhi Hong Kong Buenos Aires

**This book is dedicated to my grandson Joel.**

**Special thanks to reading consultant Dr. Linda B. Gambrell, Director of the School of Education at Clemson University, past president of the National Reading Conference, and past board member of the International Reading Association.**

**Permission to use the following photographs is gratefully acknowledged:**
**Front cover, title page: Science Photo Library, Photo Researchers, Inc.; pages 2–3, 6–7, 14–17, 26–31: National Space Science Data Center; pages 8–9: The Team Leader, Prof. Bruce C. Murray and National Space Science Data Center; pages 10–11: Dr. Robert W. Carslon, The Galileo Project and National Space Science Data Center; pages 12–13: The Principal Investigator, Dr. Frederick J. Doyle and National Space Science Data Center; pages 18–25: The Team Leader, Dr. Bradford A. Smith and National Space Science Data Center.**



ISBN 0-439-46686-5

 Published by Scholastic Inc., 557 Broadway, New York, NY 10012, by arrangement with North-South Books, Inc.


12 11 10 9 8 7 6 5 4 3 2 1 2 3 4 5 6 7/0

Printed in the U.S.A. 23

First Scholastic printing, October 2002

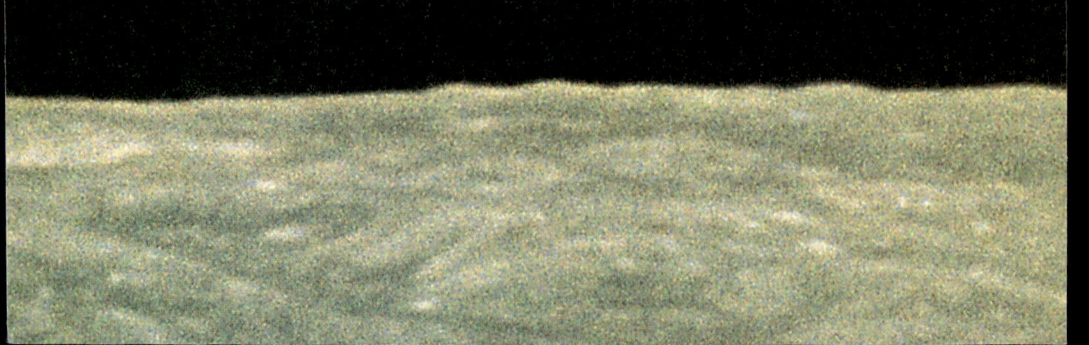

We live on a planet called Earth.

Earth is one of nine planets
that travel around the sun.
The sun and everything
that travels around it
are called the solar system.

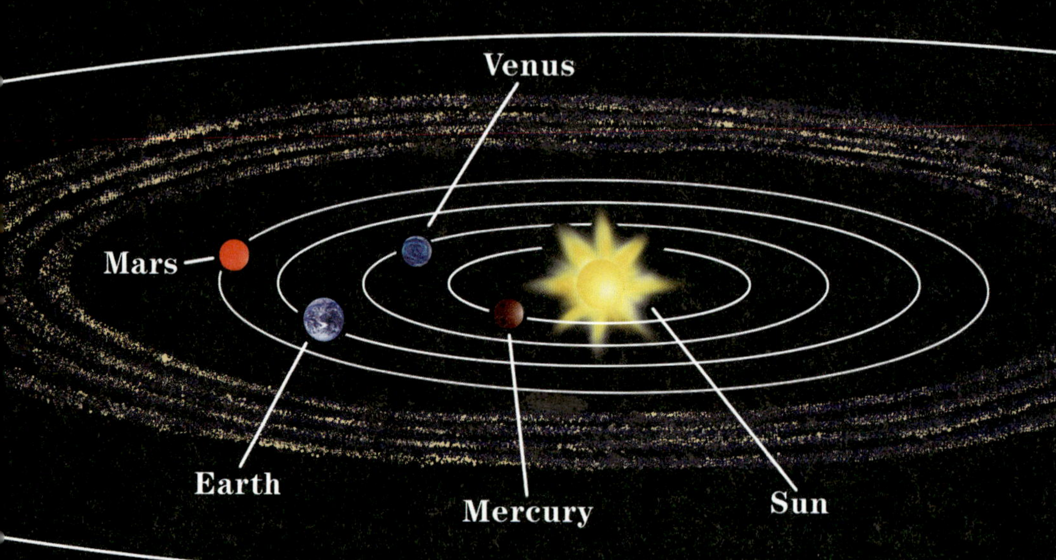

Pluto
Neptune
Uranus
Jupiter
Saturn
Asteroid Belt

The sun is a giant ball
of fiery hot gases.
If Earth were the size
of a basketball,
the sun would be as big
as a basketball court.

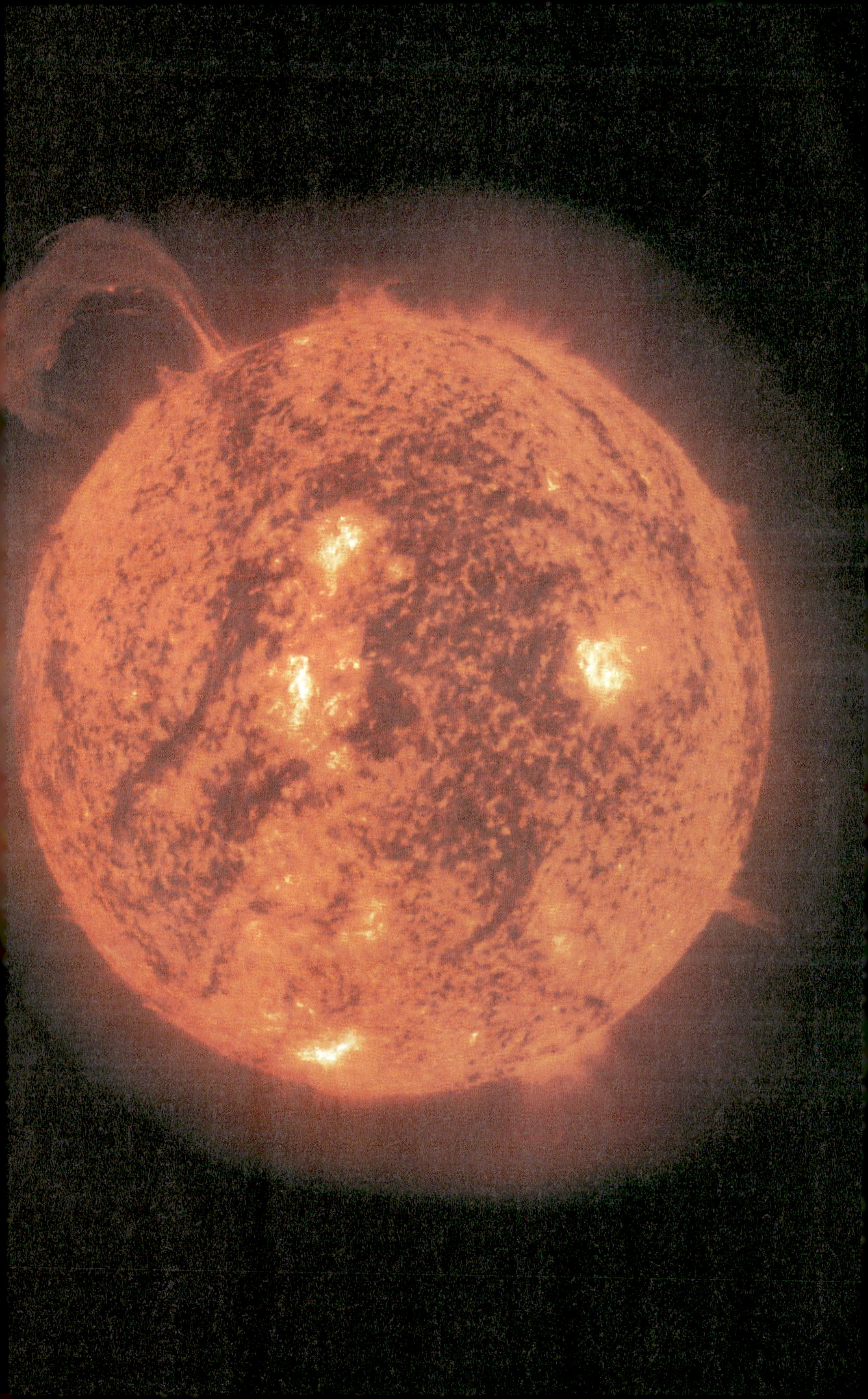

Mercury is closest to the sun. During the day, its temperature is almost 800 degrees.

But at night, the temperature drops to nearly 300 degrees below zero.

Venus is about the same size
as Earth, but it is very different.
Thick clouds cover the planet
but it has no water.
Venus is the hottest planet
in our solar system.

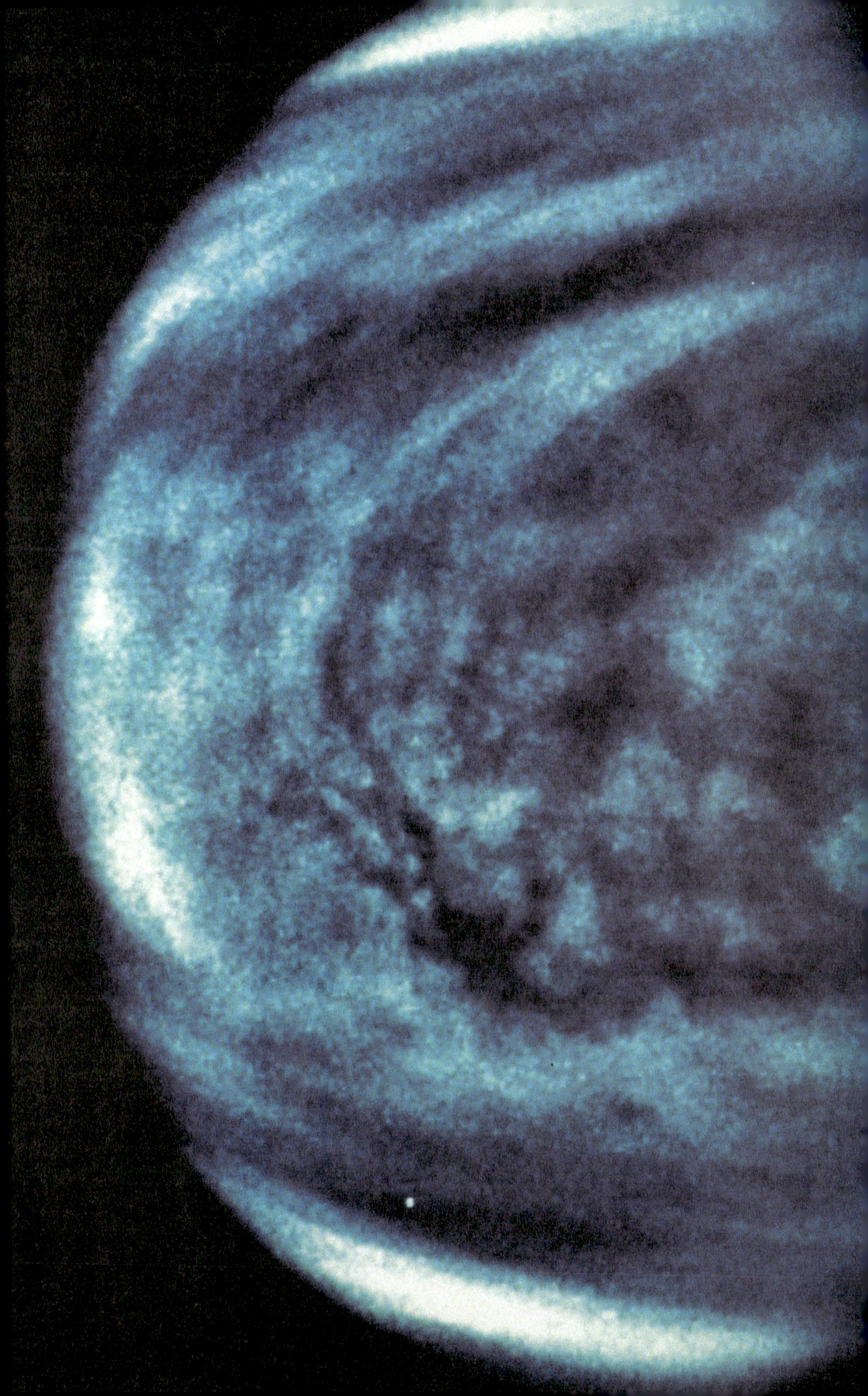

Earth is the only planet that has water on its surface.

If Earth were closer to the sun,
the oceans would boil away.
If it were farther away,
the oceans would freeze.

Earth's moon is not a planet.
Planets travel around the sun.
Moons travel around planets.
Even though Earth's moon
is 250,000 miles away,
it is our closest neighbor.

**Phases of the Moon**

new moon

crescent moon

quarter moon

gibbous moon

full moon

The surface of Mars is a red, dusty soil. Spacecraft from Earth have landed on Mars.

People are interested in looking for signs of life there. But so far they have found no signs of life.

Jupiter is much larger
than all of the other planets
combined.
The surface of Jupiter is
an ocean of liquid hydrogen
10,000 miles deep.
The Great Red Spot is
a giant storm on Jupiter.
This storm is bigger
than Earth.

Saturn is the second largest planet.
Saturn has rings made
of pieces of ice, rock, and dust.

Some pieces are smaller
than a dime.
Others are as big as a house.

Uranus is a green planet.
Its very thin rings are made
of an unknown black material.
Uranus has 5 large moons
and at least 16 smaller ones.

Neptune is a blue-green planet with giant storms on its surface. Freezing winds blow across Neptune at speeds of up to 700 miles per hour.

Pluto is the coldest planet.
It is a distant ball
of frozen gases and rock.
Some scientists think it is
too small to be called a planet.
But most people still call
Pluto the ninth planet
of our solar system.

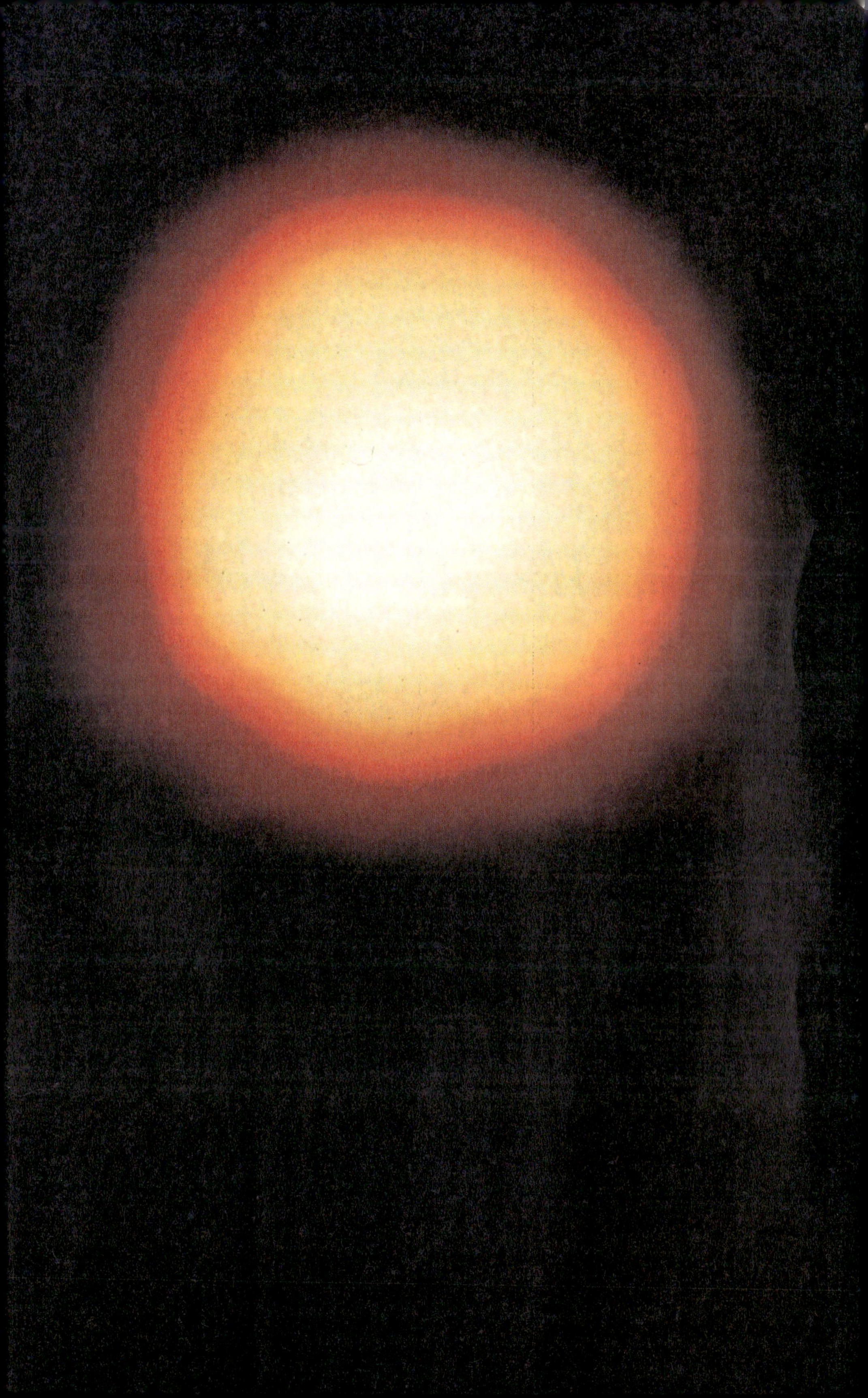

Asteroids are chunks of rock. They are much smaller than planets. About 4,000 asteroids circle the sun between Mars and Jupiter. This area is called the asteroid belt.

Far out in space, other planets circle other stars.
But no one knows if any distant planets are like Earth.
We still have much to learn about planets and stars.

| | Mercury | Venus | Earth | Mars | Jupiter | Saturn | Uranus | Neptune | Pluto |
|---|---|---|---|---|---|---|---|---|---|
| Distance from Sun (millions of miles) | 36 | 67 | 93 | 142 | 484 | 891 | 1785 | 2793 | 3647 |
| Orbital Period (days) | 88 | 225 | 365 | 687 | 4331 | 10,747 | 30,589 | 59,800 | 90,588 |
| Diameter (miles) | 3032 | 7521 | 7926 | 4222 | 88,846 | 74,897 | 31,763 | 30,775 | 1485 |
| Length of Day (hours) | 4223 | 2802 | 24 | 25 | 10 | 11 | 17 | 16 | 153 |
| Average Temperature (F) | 333 | 867 | 59 | -85 | -166 | -220 | -320 | -330 | -375 |
| Moons | 0 | 0 | 1 | 2 | 28 | 30 | 21 | 8 | 1 |
| Rings | No | No | No | No | Yes | Yes | Yes | Yes | No |